GOLDILOCKS AND THE THREE BEARS

GOLDILOCKS AND THE THREE BEARS

RETOLD AND ILLUSTRATED BY

JANET STEVENS

HOLIDAY HOUSE / NEW YORK

For BLAKE

Printed in the United States of America
First Edition

Library of Congress Cataloging-in-Publication Data

Stevens, Janet.
Goldilocks and the three bears.

SUMMARY: A little girl wanders by the home of three bears and seeing no one at home goes inside, helps herself to food, and falls asleep.
[1. Folklore. 2. Bears—Folklore] I. Title.
PZ8.1.S8572Go 1986 398.2′1 [E] 85-27312
ISBN 0-8234-0608-3

Once upon a time, deep in a forest, there lived a family of three bears. There was a great big Papa Bear, a middle-sized Mama Bear, and a little Baby Bear.

Every morning at breakfast, the three bears each ate a steaming bowl of porridge. Papa Bear had a great big appetite, so he ate from a great big bowl. Mama Bear had a middle-sized appetite, so she ate from a middle-sized bowl. And Baby Bear had a little baby appetite, so he ate from a little baby bowl.

After breakfast, the three bears each sat in a special chair. Papa Bear was so big that he sat in a great big chair. Mama Bear was middle-sized, so she sat in a middle-sized chair. And Baby Bear was so little that he sat in a little baby rocking chair all his own.

At night, when they went to sleep, the three bears each slept in a special bed. Papa Bear was so big that he slept in a great big bed. Mama Bear was middle-sized, so she slept in a middle-sized bed. And Baby Bear was so little that he slept in a little baby bed all his own.

One morning, when the bears sat down to breakfast, their porridge was so hot that it burned their tongues. They decided to leave it on the table to cool while they went for a walk in the forest.

While they were gone, a little girl named Goldilocks wandered by their house. When she smelled the porridge, she walked up to the window and peeked in. She saw the three bowls of porridge on the table. *Mmmmmmm*, did they smell good. No one seemed to be home, so Goldilocks went inside.

She walked right over to the table and tasted the porridge in the biggest bowl.

"Ouch!" she cried. "This is much too hot!"

She tasted the porridge in the middle-sized bowl.

"Oh, no!" she cried. "This is much too cold!"

Then she tasted the porridge in the little baby bowl. It was not too hot and it was not too cold. It was just right. It tasted so good that Goldilocks ate it all up.

Goldilocks was feeling very full so she decided to sit and rest before returning home. She sat down on the great big chair.

"Ouch!" she cried. "This is much too hard!"

She sat on the middle-sized chair.

"Oh, no!" she cried. "This is much too soft!"

Then she sat in the little baby rocking chair. It was not too hard and it was not too soft. It was just right. Goldilocks rocked and rocked.

But she rocked so hard that,
CRASH,
the chair broke.

Goldilocks fell
to the floor.
KERPLUNK.

Goldilocks felt so sore and tired that she went upstairs to take a nap.

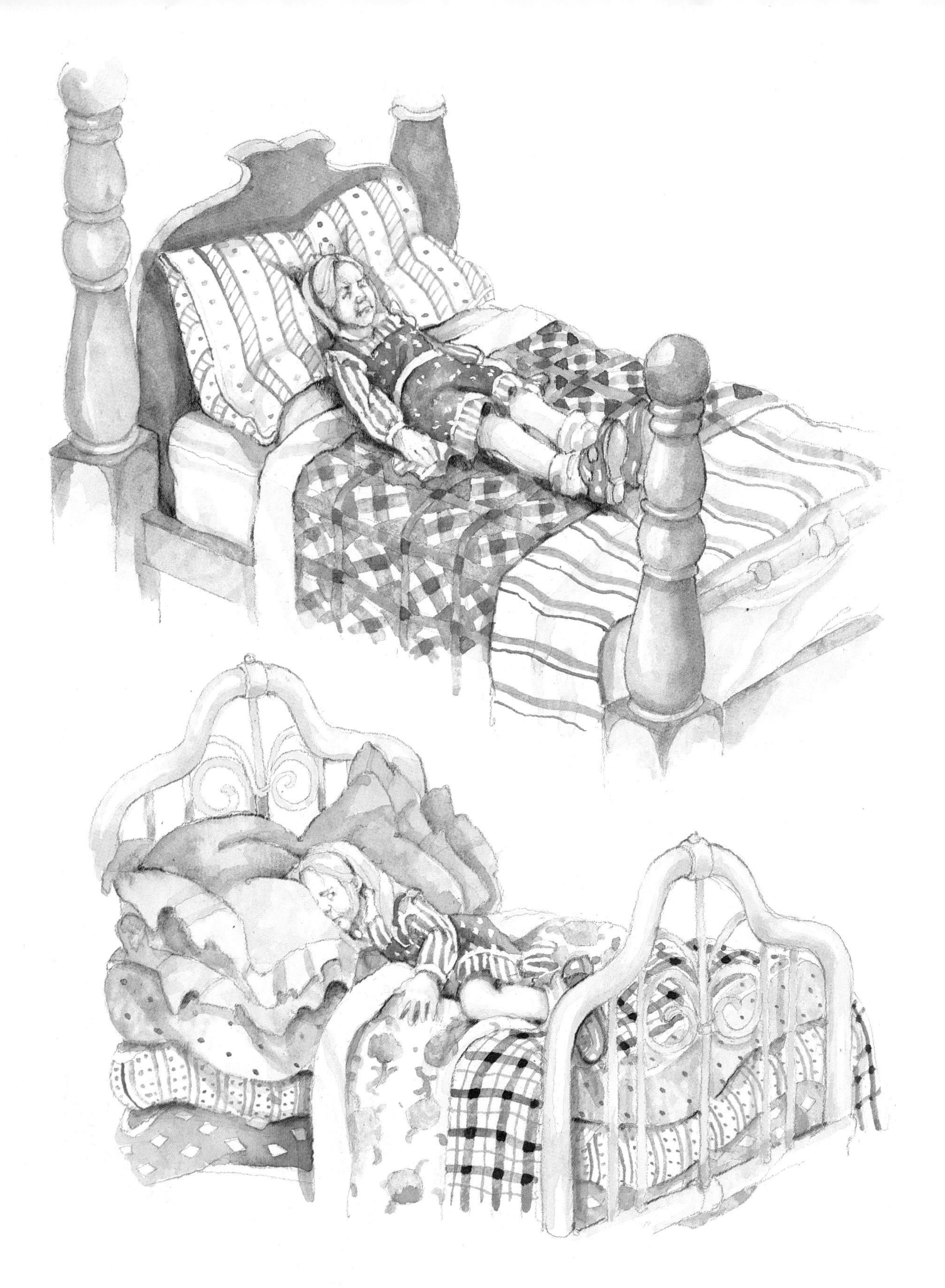

She lay down on the great big bed.
"Ouch!" she cried. "This is much too hard!"
She lay on the middle-sized bed.
"Oh, no!" she cried. "This is much too soft!"

Then she lay on the little baby bed. It was not too hard and it was not too soft. It was just right. Goldilocks crawled under the covers and fell asleep.

The three bears returned home to finish their breakfast. Papa Bear looked at his porridge.

"Someone has been eating my porridge," he growled in his great big voice.

"Someone has been eating my porridge, too," said Mama Bear in her middle-sized voice.

"Someone has been eating my porridge and has eaten it all up!" squeaked Baby Bear in his little baby voice.

After breakfast, Papa Bear went to sit in his chair. But something was different!

"Someone has been sitting in my chair," Papa Bear growled in his great big voice.

"Someone has been sitting in my chair, too," said Mama Bear in her middle-sized voice.

"Someone has been sitting in my chair, and, look, it's all broken!" squeaked Baby Bear in his little baby voice.

Then the three bears went upstairs. Papa Bear frowned and looked at his bed.

"Someone has been sleeping in my bed," he growled in his great big voice.

"Someone has been sleeping in my bed, too," said Mama Bear in her middle-sized voice.

"Someone has been sleeping in my bed, and here she is!" squeaked Baby Bear in his little baby voice.

Goldilocks woke up. When she saw the three bears, she leaped out of bed, ran down the stairs, and flew out the door.

Goldilocks ran and ran. "I'm never going to wander alone in the forest again," she said when she got home.

And that suited the three bears just fine!